HOW MANY
GREEKS
CAN YOU FIT INSIDE
A HORSE?

Dr Dino's Learnatorium

DINO

Published by Dino Books,
an imprint of John Blake Publishing Ltd,
3 Bramber Court, 2 Bramber Road,
London W14 9PB, England

www.johnblakebooks.com

www.facebook.com/johnblakebooks 🔲
twitter.com/jblakebooks 🔲

This edition published in 2015

ISBN: 978 1 78418 654 8

British Library Cataloguing-in-Publication Data:

A catalogue record for this book is available from the British Library.

Design by www.envydesign.co.uk

Printed in Great Britain by CPI Group (UK) Ltd

1 3 5 7 9 10 8 6 4 2

Papers used by John Blake Publishing are natural, recyclable products made
from wood grown in sustainable forests. The manufacturing processes conform
to the environmental regulations of the country of origin.

Every attempt has been made to contact the relevant copyright-holders,
but some were unobtainable. We would be grateful if the
appropriate people could contact us.

Introduction

Welcome, children, to my wonderful learnatorium. This is a place that holds all of the knowledge in the universe – a little like the Internet, but without all of the distracting videos of cats. If this isn't your first time in my learnatorium then you will know that, along with my loyal Assistant Learnatours, I am a dinosaur devoted to science, and to teaching you all of the interesting facts that your teachers either don't know or don't want to tell you.

This, however, is a book of myths and legends – the opposite of facts and science! So why would I, Dr Dino, with a PhD in Universal Knowledge, be interested in these stories? Well, partly because a culture's myths and legends give you a great insight into their psychology. The Germans, for example, love to tell stories with morals to their children to frighten them into being well-behaved, while the Japanese... well, the Japanese are just scared of monsters. But apart from that, some of these are just great stories!

From gruesome mythological creatures (most of whom

want to kill you for one reason or another) to bizarre stories of ridiculous gods, this is a collection of legends that you will definitely find interesting and intriguing. Unfortunately, because I have such limited space in this book, I could only give you a very small sample of all of the myths and legends out there. But hopefully you will want to do some research of your own... if you do, you are always welcome at my learnatorium!

And who knows, maybe some of the stories are even true... after all I am a talking T-rex!

Japanese

'GODZILLA IS COMING!!!'

The Japanese have an extremely unfair idea that enormous walking scaly green reptiles are something to be afraid of. If they met me they would see that we are really very gentle creatures and wouldn't hurt a fly! Unless it's a mealtime, in which case my stomach sometimes gets the better of me...

Godzilla isn't actually a dinosaur. In fact, its name means 'Gorilla-Whale', which is a bit confusing because it looks like neither a gorilla, nor a whale. However, the famous Japanese monster is supposedly descended from dinosaurs and spent millions of years lurking in the depths of the ocean until nuclear radiation released during World War Two mutated it into the creature that has destroyed Japan and Tokyo dozens of times.

Of course, Godzilla isn't real... but that hasn't stopped it starring in twenty-eight films (and counting) and having its own star on Hollywood's Walk of Fame. Shinjuku, in Tokyo, even had a ceremony to honour Godzilla and make it an 'official cultural ambassador' – despite Godzilla destroying Shinjuku three times in movies!

Although Godzilla is the most famous of them, the Japanese believe in more than one monster stalking their

islands. In fact, if you listen to all of their tall stories you might think you can't leave home without bumping into a demon or worse. But here are five of the strangest:

5. If you ever find yourself in a public toilet in Japan, avoid using the last stall at all costs. Because if you do, while you are sitting there you could receive a visit from the Aka Manto, a devilish demon who haunts the loo while bizarrely wearing a cape and a mask.

He will stick his hand under the door and ask you if you want red or blue toilet paper. Choose the red… and he'll slice you up until your clothes are red! Choose the blue… and he'll strangle you until your face is blue! And choose anything else… he'll drag you down into the underworld with him. It's a bit of a lose-lose-lose situation really. The only way out of it is to say 'no paper.'

4. Traditionally, Japanese houses had walls made of paper, and the Moku-mokuren are relatively harmless spirits that live inside these walls. If the paper gets ripped then the Mokumokuren's eyes can be seen watching everything you do from the holes in the walls… creepy!

But, at least one traveller is said to have kept his head, and eyes, about him when he slept one night in

an abandoned building. He woke up to see hundreds of eyes staring down at him, and instead of running away like a normal person he took out his knife, cut the eyes from the walls and sold them to an eye doctor for a tidy profit.

3. The Kappa are turtle-like river demons that are very polite and friendly... until they trick you into getting in the water, where they drown you and suck your blood! Fortunately, there are a couple of easy ways to get rid of a Kappa.

The first is that they get their power from a small cup of water on the tops of their heads, and if it spills they become paralysed. A good trick if you see one is to bow to them – they are so polite that they are forced to bow back and the water goes sloshing out.

The second is they have a secret weakness... for cucumbers! It's the only food they like more than blood, and if you give them one not only will they spare your life, they'll even grant you favours. So, if you're planning to go for a quick dip, best to bring your veg with you.

Modern Monsters

Most countries have a history littered with myths and legends, but very few still come up with new ones every day. Japan is one of them – even the legend of Godzilla is only sixty years old. The Teke Teke, for example, is the spirit of a young girl who recently fell in front of a train and was cut in half, and now she crawls around with a wicked scythe, looking for young victims to slice in half to join her.

That might seem unbelievable, but it seems Japanese people are very gullible. In the 1970s, the Kuchisake-Onna was rumoured to be wandering the streets, looking for victims. She is the ghost of a woman who had her mouth cut from ear to ear. Wearing a mask to hide her wound, she roams around until she finds a young child and then asks if she is pretty. If the child says no then the ghost takes out a pair of scissors and kills them. If the child says yes, the Kuchisake-Onna takes off her mask, revealing her gashed mouth, and asks the same question again. If the child changes their mind and says no, she kills them. If they say yes… then she cuts their mouth so that it looks like hers! Quite an evil ghost, as ghosts go.

Despite the fact that there aren't any Japanese children running around with cuts in their mouths, the gullible Japanese were so scared of the Kuchisake-Onna that during the height of the rumoured sightings in the 1970s, schoolteachers actually walked their schoolchildren home to protect them from her!

2. The Bake-Kujira, which translates to 'ghost-whale', is a huge 20-metre-long whale. Which isn't too uncommon in Japan, except that this whale is dead. The rotting car-cass is just a skeleton

with stinking flesh hanging off it – a truly gruesome sight. The Bake-Kujira is said to be incredibly aggressive, attacking whaling ships whenever it spots them and, what's worse, if you fire a harpoon at it, it will just sail through without doing any damage.

But worst of all, if you are unlucky enough to spot one, but lucky enough to survive the encounter, then a curse comes down on your entire village, bringing famine and plague with it. Maybe it's better just to die!

1. The most bizarre mythological creature in all of Japan, if not in the entire world, is the Akaname, whose name translates as 'filth-licker'. He is a little goblin-like demon who, like the Aka Manto, loves to hang around in bathrooms. This slimy, naked creature crawls around the bathroom at night and licks up any grime, dirt… or worse… that it finds in a toilet.

While this is truly disgusting, it might seem like a pretty good idea to have something come in and clean your bathroom while you sleep. Unfortunately, his tongue is poisonous, so the more he laps up, the more likely you are to catch a horrible disease. Best to do the scrubbing up yourself I think!

The Maori

The Maori people arrived in New Zealand on canoes (they must have been big canoes!) in the thirteenth century, and brought with them a Polynesian (a term we scientists use for the small islands dotted around the Pacific Ocean) mythology to describe the world around them – things like the sun and the moon, the wind, death, the seasons – that is poetic, beautiful and incredibly unscientific. As someone with a PhD in Universal Knowledge, I find it exceedingly annoying, but I do understand that not everyone has access to my wonderful learnatorium so I have to make allowances.

The Birth of New Zealand

Maui was the youngest in a family of boys, and longed for the day he could go out fishing with his brothers. They would tease him, saying that he was too little, and so skinny that they would mistake him for a piece of bait and throw him overboard. However, Maui had a secret – he possessed magic. And this is where the story gets better.

He took a mystical jawbone he had lying around and made a magic fishing line with it, snuck onto his brothers' waka (boat) and went out to sea with them. When he revealed himself to them they were angry with him and blamed him for their lack of success at fishing that day. They wanted to take him home, so he cast a spell that meant that the shore seemed further away than it actually was, and they continued rowing out to sea. It only made things worse when he took out his ridiculous jawbone fishing line and asked his brothers for bait.

They made fun of him and wouldn't give him anything to use, so he punched his own nose and smeared his blood all over the jawbone before hurling it into the ocean. His brothers were howling with laughter, but soon stopped when the line went taut and Maui snagged the biggest fish any of them had ever seen.

After a huge battle between Maui and the fish, he dragged it to the surface and it turned out to be the biggest fish the world had ever seen. While Maui went home to get help with the fish, his brothers began arguing over who would get credit for the catch and the fight turned violent – they began smashing each other and the fish, taking huge chunks out of it.

In the end, the fish was too huge to move, and over time it became the North Island of New Zealand, with the gashes and mounds the brothers had created becoming the valleys and mountains. The waka the brothers went out in became the South Island, and that's how New Zealand came to be.

And if you know any fishermen, who are known for exaggerating, with a taller tale than that, I will be very surprised!

Irish

Ireland is a wild land, and it was once populated by huge giants, the most famous of whom was Fionn MacCumhail. He lived a fairly exciting life and had many adventures, but he is best known for being the person who created the Isle of Man and the Giant's Causeway – a group of huge rocks off the coast of Ireland.

Of course, you and I both know that a) giants never existed and b) both the Isle of Man and the Giant's Causeway were created by well-known geographical phenomena. Not, as the legend goes, when Fionn ripped up part of Ireland to hurl at an approaching enemy and missed, thus creating the Isle of Man. But this is a book of myth and legend, not of fact and science, so here is the story of how Fionn created the Giant's Causeway:

Fionn MacCumhail wanted to get across the sea to Scotland, but as a giant he wasn't a great swimmer, and he didn't particularly want to get his feet wet, so instead

he ripped up a number of large rocks and began building a bridge of stepping stones – the Giant's Causeway – to get across.

However, as he was working he heard the approach of a truly giant Scottish giant called Benandonner, who was so enormous he made Fionn look puny. Benandonner wasn't impressed with Fionn's bridge and was spoiling for a fight, much like when two T-rex used to meet back in the good old days. Fionn panicked, and didn't know what to do... If he fought, he was sure to lose, and have you ever been on the wrong side of a giant's punch? It's not a pleasant experience.

Fortunately, his wife Oona was close by, and the clever Fionn dressed himself up as a baby. When Benandonner came looking for him, Oona told him Fionn wasn't there, but his baby was – would he like to see him? Benandonner took one look at the 'baby' and was terrified. If Fionn's baby was that big, then how big would he be? He turned tail and fled, leaving a relieved Fionn behind.

Sensibly, Fionn decided to abandon his stepping stone project, and the Giant's Causeway will forever be there, just off the coast of Ireland, as proof.

The Salmon of Knowledge and Little Fionn

Confusingly, Fionn MacCumhail isn't a giant in all Irish legends, but he is clever, and a great warrior and leader. But he wasn't born that way...

As a young boy Fionn was sent to live with Finnegas, a wise poet who was constantly hunting the Salmon of Knowledge – so-called because the salmon had eaten hazelnuts from the Well of Wisdom (don't even ask about the Well of Wisdom!). Whoever ate the salmon was destined to gain all of the knowledge in the world... so they would almost be as smart as I am, thanks to my learnatorium!

Finally, after eight years of searching, Finnegas spotted the salmon and pounced, using all of his energy in a great battle to capture it. He was so tired from his efforts that he ordered Fionn to cook it for him, but not to eat even a nibble of it. Fionn obeyed of course, as any good student should do to their teacher (as long as those teachers are really wise – not like some of your teachers probably are at school!), but as he checked to see if the salmon was cooked through he got a drop of boiling oil on his thumb.

In pain, he immediately sucked on his thumb, and straight away wisdom and knowledge coursed through him. Finnegas saw this and made him eat the whole thing, which gave Fionn knowledge that only I, the great Dr Dino, can match.

You can only imagine how angry Finnegas was after spending so many years of his life searching for the Salmon of Knowledge!

Leprechauns are the most famous mythological creatures in Ireland. These little sprites keep mainly to themselves, spending their time mending shoes or hiding pots of gold at the end of rainbows. However, they are incredibly mischievous (possibly because they are often drunk – although not as much as their lesser known cousins the Clurichaun, who are almost the same as Leprechauns, except their sole reason to be is

to drink alcohol and cause drunken destruction!) and play tricks on farmers and villagers, such as riding on the backs of their sheep or dogs at night to move them to unexpected places.

They generally bear no ill will to humans, although that didn't help the poor woman who was once captured by a group of them and, because of their love of music and dancing, was forced to dance so much over the next eight years that her toes fell off! However, they are by no means the only mythological creature wandering the Irish countryside, although they are the only ones that will grant you three wishes if you capture them.

Banshees are best avoided at all costs. These fairy women can be heard wailing across the fields of rural Ireland, and if you spot one then it means someone in your family is sure to die. Even King James I was said to have seen one just before his death.

The Abhartach is something like a vampire-dwarf – effectively an evil dwarf who sucks blood. Our hero Fionn was the first to kill one of these, only for it to come back to life the next day seeking more victims. The only way to subdue it for good is to bury it upside-down head-first.

If you ever see a Leprechaun wearing red, beware. It is most likely a Far Darrig. These little creatures are said to have been men who wandered into the world of fairies by accident, and now spend their days warning other people from making the same mistake. They are fairly grumpy though, and tend to do irritating things like give humans nightmares and fool them into carrying corpses along roads for miles, thinking they are something other than dead bodies.

However, if one comes to your door in the dead of night, do let it in for a cup of tea. If you make it angry with you, it has the habit of switching babies for changelings – the children of fairies who are pretty mischievous themselves to say the least!

The Caoranach isn't a monster you will have to worry about on a trip to Ireland because St Patrick slew her after a two-day battle centuries ago (and also she's mythical, so was never actually real in the first place). The Caoranach lived in a lair that was said to be the gateway to the underworld, and she gave birth to demons and devils by the dozen, who would terrorise the nearby villagers. Fortunately, St Patrick put paid to her in an epic fight, and rumour has it at one point he allowed himself to be swallowed whole by the fiendish

beast before hacking his way out from the inside with a crucifix.

It's stories like that which remind me to always make sure I chew my animals properly when I'm eating, rather than just swallow them whole. It's unlikely a cow will do to me what St Patrick did to the Caoranach, but you can never be too careful.

Ancient Egyptians

Like me, the Ancient Egyptians were smarter, more civilized and more cultured than anyone else in the world at the time. While they were building enormously complex stone pyramids and statues in the warmth of the desert, pretty much everyone else was freezing their butts off in mud huts – if they were lucky!

However, for all of my respect for their scientific and technological prowess, they still believed things that no dinosaur in his (or her) right mind could think were true.

The Egyptian gods were a pretty ugly bunch – and that's coming from a Tyrannosaurus rex! In general, they were normal humans from the shoulders down, but with the heads of animals on top. Khnum, the God of the Nile River, was no different because he had the head of a ram, and just to make things a little weirder, his head was green.

Despite these apparent disadvantages, the Egyptians

had great respect for Khnum. They believed he sat at his potter's wheel all day crafting little human babies out of the Nile's clay before magically implanting them in the wombs of soon-to-be mothers. I can almost see where they were coming from... the Nile was the source of life in the dry Egyptian desert. But as a scientist I have to put my claw down at the idea of being made of clay.

A Trip to the Underworld

Se-Osiris was the greatest magician Egypt had ever seen. When he was still a child he stood with his father Setna, who was pretty dim compared to him, and watched as two funeral processions went by. One procession, for a rich man, was expensive and filled with many priests and great offerings. The other was for a poor man, who had just a wooden coffin and his two sons to carry him.

Setna turned to his son and said, 'I hope one day to have a funeral like the rich man's.' The wise Se-Osiris was

scornful and said he hoped for just the opposite – which really annoyed his father, I can tell you! The slow-witted Setna thought his son hated him, but Se-Osiris said it was just the opposite, and that if he didn't believe him then he could take a trip with him to the Underworld to see for himself.

Now, nobody had ever been to the Underworld and lived to tell the tale, so when Setna's young son said this he must have been pretty sceptical (almost as sceptical as I am about whether this story actually happened or not...). Se-Osiris was insistent though, so they went to a temple and Se-Osiris mumbled a spell and threw down some magic powder and – hey presto! – suddenly their souls were free from their bodies and floating up in the air.

Se-Osiris (who knew a bit too much about all this for a human kid in my opinion...) told his father they had to hurry because if they were caught in the Underworld by the time the sun next came up, they would be trapped there forever. And that wouldn't be a very good ending to the story. So off they flew, swifter than an arrow from an Ethiopian's bow.

The God of Death

Anubis wasn't an Egyptian god you would have wanted to have bumped into. With the head of a jackal, he was the God of Death, and he was responsible for the Weighing of the Heart – an important ceremony that took place after you died which judged where you spent your afterlife (in much the same way as Heaven and Hell works in the Christian religion).

Another important role Anubis had was as the protector of cemeteries. During the Ancient Egyptian times, there was a real problem with jackals getting into the graveyards at night and digging up human corpses to have a midnight feast on... Yuck! As a half-jackal himself, it must have been hard for Anubis to resist the temptation for a quick human snack every now and then. And believe me, as a dinosaur who works with humans, I know how he felt...

The flying pair of souls quickly made it through Egypt and, thanks to Se-Osiris's magic, found the boat of Re that carried dead souls through the many lands of the Underworld to be judged by Anubis. Although most of the lands were peaceful and happy, there were some gruesome reminders of the violence and pain that awaited you if you failed the judging – like one poor fellow whose eye was gouged out and the empty socket used as a pivot for a door, so that every time the door opened or closed he was in excruciating pain.

Eventually, all of the newly-dead souls were brought in front of a great throne where Osiris, the greatest of the gods, and Anubis waited to judge them. Se-Osiris pointed out to his foolish father the scales on which Anubis was going to weigh their hearts, and also the two souls of the rich and poor men whose funerals they had seen.

Pretty soon it was their turn to have their hearts weighed, and the rich man stepped up first. Anubis took his heart, which must have been fairly grisly, placed it on the scales and put the Feather of Truth on the other scale. The rich man, who was pretty nervous at this point, watched in horror as the heart sank further and further until suddenly from the shadows Ammit, the Devourer of the Dead, the Eater of Hearts, who was a demon-dog, leapt up and scoffed it down. Osiris saw this and said,

'Take this man to Duat to dwell with Apep the Terrible in the Pits of Fire!' In case you're as slow as some of your teachers... the Pits of Fire aren't a great place to be.

The poor man stepped up next, and if he wasn't worried before, he certainly was now! His heart was taken by Anubis, placed on the scales and... it rose up as far as it could go. Osiris saw this and sent him into the Field of Peace, where everything he loved in the world could be found – an altogether better proposition than the Pits of Fire.

Swiftly, Se-Osiris led his father back to their bodies, and they got back just in the nick of time to see the sun rise. And to this day they are the only humans to have ever visited the realms of the dead, which I think is even more impressive when you take into account the fact that the realms of the dead don't actually exist!

Everyone knows how much the Egyptians loved their mummies! Even your history teacher could probably tell you that the rulers of Egypt were called pharaohs and were embalmed and buried in the great pyramids. But they weren't the only mummies you could find in Ancient Egypt.

Archaeologists have found thousands of mummified animals – everything from cats and birds to crocodiles and monkeys were wrapped up and buried. The Egyptians did this for a number of reasons: sometimes as offerings to the gods, sometimes so the human mummy could eat the animal mummy in the afterlife, and sometimes just because the animal was the favourite pet of the dead human! And the Egyptians really did love their pets. In fact, cats were considered so sacred that to kill one was punishable by death!

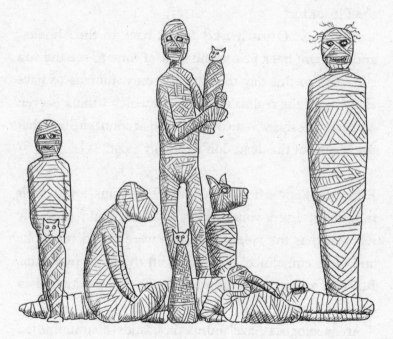

Germans

One of my favourite countries to visit is Germany. There they have a great appreciation for science, order and learning – three of the most important aspects of my learnatorium. However, I have met more than one human child in my time and I know that, unlike dinosaur kids, they are not always the best-behaved. Science, order and learning are not often as high on the list of importance to them as fun, games and causing mischief.

Fortunately, the Germans have a way to teach their children a lesson, or a 'moral'. While your parents may have read you tales like *Little Red Riding Hood*, *Snow White* or *Sleeping Beauty*, the Germans have *Der Struwwelpeter*, which means Shock-Headed Peter. That may sound like a boring name for a book but the stories, and their lessons, are anything but. Here's a brief description of some of the most gruesome:

The Dreadful Story of the Matches – Little Harriet was left at home one day by her mum. Harriet noticed a box of matches on the table, but she knew she wasn't allowed to play with them. However, she thought the flame was pretty, so she grabbed the box and made to light one. Her cats tried to stop her… but they were only cats, so what could they do? She lit one and laughed with joy. But instead of putting it out, the flame caught her apron, which burst on fire. Quickly the rest of her clothes caught fire, then her arms, her face, her hair… everything. And when her mother came back all she found were her shoes lying in a pile of ashes.

Moral of the Story: If you disobey your parents and play with matches, YOU WILL DIE!

The Story of Bad Frederick – Frederick was a vicious little boy. He loved torturing animals and spent his days tearing the wings off flies, breaking birds' wings and throwing kittens downstairs. In short, he wasn't very nice. One day, he took a whip to his dog, so his dog turned around and bit his leg – and not just a little nip either, he almost bit right through the bone. To make matters worse, while Frederick was in bed recovering, his dog ate all of his food and he couldn't get up to stop him.

Moral of the Story: Don't torture animals. They can bite back HARD (trust me, I'm a T-rex).

The Story of the Thumb-Sucker – Conrad loved to suck his thumb. One day his mother warned him: 'Stop sucking your thumb, little Conrad, because the tall tailor will come with his great scissors and chop them off, if you're not careful.' Conrad thought, not unreasonably, that there was no such thing as a tailor who chopped off little boys' thumbs. So, as soon as his mum had turned her back he popped his thumb back into his mouth. Immediately, the door burst open and the tailor stood there, scissors at the ready, and with two quick snips he chopped Conrad's thumbs right off.

Moral of the Story: Don't suck your thumbs, or else someone will CHOP THEM OFF!

The Story of Augustus Who Wouldn't Eat His Soup – Augustus was a chubby chap who loved his food, especially his soup. One day he decided to be a little naughty and threw his soup on the floor, shouting 'Take the nasty soup away!' He decided there and then that he wouldn't ever eat soup again. Unfortunately for him, that was all his parents had. For five days they served him soup, and for five days Augustus threw it on the floor. Augustus grew thinner and thinner until eventually he starved to death.

Moral of the Story: Eat what your parents tell you or else YOU WILL DIE!

The Germans, it seems, don't really believe in 'happily ever after'! And it's not just their fairy tales that are horrific either. The mythological creatures that live in Germany don't sound like you would like to meet them for a nice cup of tea and a friendly chat either, like...

The Nachzehrer is a sort of vampire – but maybe even worse! Nachzehrers don't need to be bitten to become Nachzehrers. Instead, when someone dies of the plague they might become one, which isn't much of a problem now but in medieval times it was a serious possibility. You could apparently tell if the plague-victim was going to change because it would lie in its grave with the left eye open.

When they came back to life they would rise up out of their coffins and come after the rest of their family, causing them to fall sick and die, before feasting on them in their graves... at least the Nachzehrer would wait until after they were dead to eat them!

The only way to stop them is to put a coin in their mouths and chop off their heads – anything less than that and they will still just come back to life, ready to eat their family until there are none left.

The Erdhenne – which translates as Earth Hen – is one of the friendlier inhabitants of Germany. For a start, it's just a chicken, which isn't very frightening at all. Supposedly, one can be found in most farmhouses in the country and normally they are a help to the family living there, clucking loudly whenever danger is coming. However, if anyone should ever catch sight of the Erdhenne then they will be dead within the year.

The (kind-of) Friendly Giant

Not all German mythological creatures are that bad…
some are just mischievous, like Rubezahl the shape-
shifting giant. There are many stories about him and,
as with most German stories, they have a moral:
Don't Trust Shape-Shifting Giants!

He once changed himself into a mound so that
when a travelling glass salesman sat on him for a
rest, he vanished, causing all of his glass to smash.
Rubezahl felt bad though, so he changed himself into
a donkey and let the glass salesman sell him to a
miller for more than the glass was worth. Then he
simply ran off… leaving the miller fairly unhappy, but
the glass salesman laughing all the way to the bank.

Another time he made some fine-quality pigs out of
straw with magic, and sold them to a farmer at a
very good price with the instructions not to let them
go near water. The farmer thought he was getting a

bargain, so he bought them. The problem with pigs, though, is that they like to roll around in mud, and these pigs were no different. So the farmer, ignoring Rubezahl's seemingly ridiculous warning, drove them to a river to get clean. No sooner had they hit the water than they turned back into straw and floated away, leaving the farmer out of luck.

Once while wandering the woods that belonged to a particularly tyrannical lord, Rubezahl ran into a peasant who had been told he had to carry an oak tree back to the lord's mansion all by himself, and if he didn't he would be in serious trouble (and remember this is a country where they cut off your thumbs just for sucking them!). Of course, this was impossible for a human – you are so weak compared to dinosaurs – so the peasant was distraught. Rubezahl told him to go home and not to worry, and then he threw the oak tree right into the lord's front garden, blocking the front door. It turned out that the tree was so big, the lord and all his men couldn't move it either, and the lord had to knock a whole wall down to make a new entrance to his house!

What happened to you the last time you snuck out of bed after your bedtime? Were you grounded? Scolded, perhaps? If you lived in Germany, you might have to deal with the Nachtkrapp – a vicious giant Night Raven that flies around in the darkness searching for its prey: little human children. And when it spots one up after its bedtime it will swoop down, grab it with its talons and

fly back to its nest where it sets about devouring the tasty morsel. First, it rips the child apart limb by limb, then it pecks out the heart before gulping the remains down in one.

Moral of the Story: If you stay up past your bedtime then YOU WILL DIE!

I told you the Germans liked their morals.

Aztecs

If your teachers have taught you anything about the Aztecs, it's probably that they were a powerful tribe who lived in Mexico about 600 years ago who built huge pyramids and – what they are most famous for – practised a lot of human sacrifice. You might think it's a pretty odd thing to do, sacrificing another human to the gods, and to be honest you would be right. In my opinion, the only reason to kill a human being is if you're hungry (and I stopped doing that centuries ago, I promise...). So why did the Aztecs do it?

The Creation Myth

We live in the fifth Age of Creation. The previous four ages had come and gone, meaning that the world had been created and destroyed four times already. The Aztec gods had all gathered to start the fifth Age – they had the world and the sun ready to go, but they needed one of their number to sacrifice themselves by leaping into a huge fire in order to start the sun moving.

Tecuciztecatl was the strongest and most powerful of them, so he offered to take the plunge, but at the last minute he chickened out. Nanahuatl, one of the weakest of all the gods, saw this, closed his eyes and leapt. He was burned to a crisp in an instant, but the sun immediately creaked into action. You would have thought Tecuciztecatl would have been counting his lucky stars, but in fact he was deeply ashamed… so ashamed in fact that he jumped in himself. What a waste!

So now the earth had two suns. The other gods, however, were angry with Tecuciztecatl for trying to pretend he was as brave as Nanahuatl, when he was

actually a bit of a coward. Therefore, they found a huge rabbit (which is probably the weirdest part of this story) and threw it at Tecuciztecatl, knocking his sun to the side and putting out its flames. It became the moon, and the rabbit left an imprint on it which can still be seen (the craters that we call the Man on the Moon).

Because the gods made so many sacrifices, the Aztecs believed they had to make sacrifices of their own – human sacrifices – to appease the gods and keep the world balanced. Which is a bit more extreme than saying some Our Fathers and Hail Marys to make up for being naughty, I'm sure you'll agree!

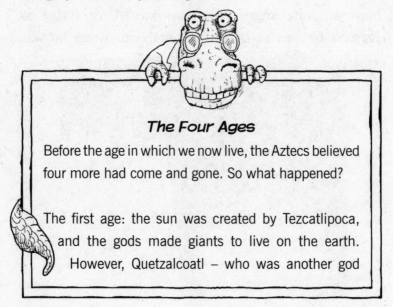

The Four Ages

Before the age in which we now live, the Aztecs believed four more had come and gone. So what happened?

The first age: the sun was created by Tezcatlipoca, and the gods made giants to live on the earth. However, Quetzalcoatl – who was another god and looked like a feathery snake – was jealous and fought Tezcatlipoca, knocking the sun from the sky in the process. Furious his creation had been destroyed, Tezcatlipoca sent a jaguar to eat all of the giants.

The second age: Quetzalcoatl created a new sun, and ruled peacefully for a time. Humans were created for the first time, but Tezcatlipoca was jealous, and turned all of the humans into monkeys, destroying the new creations. Quetzalcoatl was so angry that he sent a hurricane to blow all of the unwanted monkeys away.

The third age: Tlaloc, the god of rain, tried his hand at making the next sun. All was going well until that nuisance of a god Tezcatlipoca stole Tlaloc's wife away. Tlaloc was heartbroken and, instead of going after his wife, decided to take it out on the earth – he refused to let it rain, and then when the people begged he sent a rain of fire which burned his creation to ashes.

The fourth age: Tlaloc's sister Calchiuhtlicue was the fourth god-creator. This time Tezcatlipoca and Quetzalcoatl decided rather than fight they should join forces. Unfortunately, they only worked together to destroy the sun and flood the earth, turning everyone who lived there into a fish.

The fifth age: This is the one we live in now, and long may it last! The Aztecs believed that the earth would be destroyed by a series of powerful earthquakes, and even worked out when it would happen... 2012!

So as long as their maths isn't as bad as their science, we should be in the clear!

Why All the Human Sacrifice?

No, madam, it's not too much. You look lovely!

The Egyptians weren't the only ones whose gods were pretty ugly – all of the Aztec gods looked pretty frightening and Coatlicue – the god who was the mother of the earth – was no exception. She had a skirt made of wriggling snakes and a necklace of human hearts and skulls… which is pretty gross, even by Aztec standards!

Coatlicue was supposedly the mother of four hundred sons and one daughter, Coyolxauhqui, all of whom were gods themselves, and who were the stars and the moon. One day, she was sweeping when she found a ball of hummingbird feathers, which she tucked under her skirt. Somehow, this ball of feathers impregnated her, and when her sons and daughter heard, they were jealous. Goaded on by their sister, Coyolxhauhqui, Coatlicue's children decided to kill her.

When Coatlicue heard her children were coming, she ran, but pregnant women can't run very far (not like pregnant dinosaurs, who are almost as athletic as non-pregnant dinosaurs… just another way dinosaurs are better than humans I guess…). Soon they caught up with her on a mountainside and, just after she gave birth, they chopped off her head – which really isn't a very nice thing to do to your mother.

The newborn baby wasn't any ordinary baby though. It was Huitzilpochtli, and he came out raring for a fight. In fact, one of the first things he did was kill his half-sister Coyolxauhqui by ripping out her heart, and threw her body down the mountain. Then he chased after his brothers, driving them away from him and back to where they came from.

Huitzilpochtli became a sun-god, and every morning he rises up into the sky and drives his brothers (the stars) away again.

But why the human sacrifice? Huitzilpochtli never forgot his bloodthirsty ways and the Aztecs believed he wanted them to build mountains (pyramids) and re-create his great victory... by ripping the hearts out of defenceless humans and throwing their bodies down the sides of the 'mountain'!

Next time you and your brothers and sisters get in a fight and your parents tell you off... maybe you should just tell them they are lucky you aren't Aztecs!

Welsh

The 'Real' King Arthur

Unless you live under a rock, you will have heard tell of the glorious King Arthur and his Knights of the Round Table – incredible English heroes of old who performed unbelievable feats of daring and bravery to save maidens, kill villains, and generally act pretty cool. True English legends.

Except... they weren't actually English. In fact, King Arthur was a Welshman. And to make matters worse (or better, depending on where you are from), the original King Arthur was fighting valiantly against the Anglo-

It's just I was expecting it to be a bit bigger.

Saxons. Even the worst history teacher will be able to tell you who the Anglo-Saxons are... the English!

Over the centuries, the English realised how fantastic King Arthur and his exploits were and conveniently 'forgot' where he was from, re-writing the stories from a stiff upper-lip English point of view.

Who was it who re-wrote history in such a flagrantly ridiculous way? It was a knight called Sir Thomas Malory, who wrote *Le Morte d'Arthur* ('The Death of Arthur') in the fifteenth century. And where did he write it from...? Prison! Where he was being held for crimes ranging from burglary and armed robbery to kidnapping, extortion and even plotting to overthrow the King!

So to sum up, the glorious King Arthur – a Welsh knight who fought his entire life against the English – was re-written to be a fake English knight by a real English knight who was vicious, violent and corrupt. If King Arthur wasn't a completely made-up legend, I think he would be turning in his grave! So it's a good job he was never real in the first place.

Canrig Bwt

Hundreds of years ago, the witch Canrig Bwt sold her soul to the devil in order to gain great power. She lived under a stone bridge in Llanberis (as a dinosaur who likes to be comfortable I have always wondered  why, if she was so powerful, she chose to live under a bridge...?) and she had a very particular appetite. She would only eat the brains from freshly killed human children!

Needless to say, the people who lived nearby weren't too happy about having a brain-munching witch living just around the corner, but she was too powerful to be destroyed. Everyone who tried died in the attempt. Then one day a young farm labourer called Idwal said, 'If someone lends me a sword, I'll give it a go.' The lord of the manor was all too happy to let someone do his job for him, so he lent him his sword and sent him one night to do battle. When Idwal arrived at the witch's lair a gruesome sight met him – the bones of hundreds of little children lay everywhere, the moonlight glinting off the few curls of hair that were still left on the otherwise empty skulls.

In horror and rage, Idwal screamed at Canrig Bwt to come and face him. 'In a minute,' replied the horrid hag. 'I'm just finishing up my supper!' And before Idwal's very eyes, Canrig Bwt – with blood already running down her misshapen green face – sucked up a great slimy mass of brains. Even for a carnivorous dinosaur like me... that's just disgusting!

Idwal swallowed the vomit that threatened to come up, and saw his chance. While Canrig Bwt was busy chewing away, he bravely snuck up behind her and chopped her green head right off.

The Most Famous Dog in Wales

Llewelyn the Great ruled over Gwynedd – he was a happy man. Not only was he royalty, he also had a beautiful wife, a baby son and the greatest dog a man could wish for, Gelert.

One day, Llewelyn was out hunting with his wife, leaving the baby with a nurse and Gelert for protection. Unfortunately, the nurse was quite irresponsible and took off for a walk, leaving only Gelert to mind the child. If he was a dinosaur baby then this wouldn't be a problem, because even dinosaur babies are tough. However, I have heard that human babies are weak and pathetic.

When Llewelyn returned Gelert came rushing out of the house to greet his master – covered in blood. Llewelyn and his wife rushed into the baby's room and found carnage. The room was a mess, there was blood everywhere and the cradle was overturned – but no sign of their beloved son.

Consumed by anger and grief, Llewelyn drew his sword and stabbed his favourite dog to death. As Gelert breathed his last, a cry filled the room. There, protected underneath the cradle, was the baby boy, completely safe and unharmed. Next to him was the

corpse of an enormous wolf, which Gelert had fought and defeated.

Filled with sadness, Llewelyn buried the heroic Gelert with full honours and on that spot a town grew called Beddgelert, or Gelert's Grave, so that his noble sacrifice would be remembered forever.

Ancient Greeks

The ancient Greeks were, in my humble opinion (which should certainly be listened to, seeing as I do have a PhD in Universal Knowledge), one of the greatest cultures to ever walk the earth. Well, human cultures anyway... they still have nothing on dinosaurs. Scientifically, politically, architecturally, even militarily, the Greeks were streets ahead of anyone else at the time – and mythologically they were no different.

In Greece there were enough myths and legends for every occasion: violent villains, brave heroes, foul murders, hideous monsters, terrifying tragedies and magnificent victories. The Greeks had them all. They truly were the masters of the myth, and even I, as a scientist who loves fact and despises fiction, can appreciate them. Alas, I can only provide you with a selection, but here they are:

Sisyphus was a very wily man. He was the King of Corinth and enjoyed spending his life playing tricks on everyone – including when the time came to die. Hades, the Lord of the Underworld, turned up at Sisyphus's palace to take him away and brought with him a special new pair of handcuffs for the occasion. Sisyphus simply pretended he loved the handcuffs and got Hades to demonstrate how effective they were... on himself! Unsurprisingly, Sisyphus wasn't in a rush to let the trapped god of death go free, so he stuck him in a dungeon and left him.

Without Hades there, Sisyphus couldn't die. However, nor could anyone else! Whole armies could do battle, slicing and slashing at each other, and everyone would live to get a spot of supper, a good night's sleep and then come back again the next day.

The other gods soon noticed something fishy was going on in the human realm and went to investigate. And when they discovered who had caused all the fuss, they weren't best pleased. Sisyphus was sentenced to hard labour – an eternity of it! And the labour wasn't just hard, it was horrible too. A boulder was placed at the bottom of a hill and Sisyphus had to push it to the top. The problem was that every time he made it, the boulder would just roll back down and he would have to start all over again.

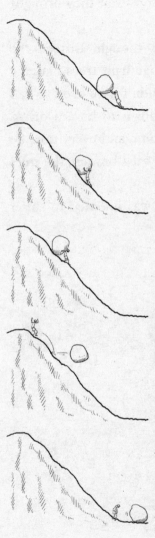

It's probably a good thing your teachers aren't so inventive with their punishments!

Sisyphus wasn't the only Greek to get a hard time from the gods. Tantalus did too, although he really deserved it. He was one of the many sons of Zeus (the head god), and he impressed the gods so much over the years that they honoured him by agreeing to come to a banquet at his house.

Tantalus, however, was a nasty demi-god, and he thought it would be a hilarious joke to kill his son Pelops, chop him up and serve him in a pie to the guests. Personally, I think he needs to work on his party-hosting skills, and it seems the Greek gods did too. They found out what had happened (luckily before tucking in to their meat surprise) and felt so sorry for Pelops that they brought him back to life.

Tantalus didn't get off lightly, though. Instead the gods threw him in a lake with huge fruit trees hanging overhead for all eternity. This wouldn't have been so bad except that every time he bent down to have a drink, the water would flow away from him, and every time he reached to pluck a ripe fruit from off a branch, the trees would sway out of his way.

And so the tantalized Tantalus was doomed to suffer for all time.

Homer's Wooden Horse

One of the greatest storytellers of all time was Homer (the Greek, not the yellow cartoon idiot). Today we still have his two epic poems in full – the *Iliad* and the *Odyssey* – which were written around 2,800 years ago and are hundreds of pages long.

The *Iliad* tells the famous story of the Greek siege of Troy, including the exploits of the hero Achilles whose only weakness was his heel (hence humans have Achilles' heels even today). Unfortunately for Achilles, a sharp shooter got him with an arrow in the heel, and he was

slain. It serves him right for being an idiot: if you knew that you could only be injured in one place... wouldn't you wear armour there?

Homer also talks about the famous Trojan horse, which is a story that I'm sure even your teachers know. To sum up, the Greeks left a huge wooden horse as a gift for the Trojans to signal their intentions to give up. Little did the Trojans know, a crack unit of Greek soldiers were hidden inside, and when their guard was down the Greeks leapt out, opened the gates and massacred the Trojans. A lovely story!

As a scientist and doctor, however, I have to tell you this simply isn't true. That tall tale came from Greek storytellers – a notorious bunch prone to embellishments or, as your parents would call them if you tried to get away with them, lies.

In fact, the wooden horse was most likely an enormous battering ram, covered in horse hide for protection, and perhaps with the ramming part shaped a bit like a horse too, for good measure. Rather than trick the Trojans into letting them in, the Greeks used this 'horse' to smash the front door in – not quite as subtle a trick.

So if anyone asks you how many Greeks fit inside the Trojan horse, the answer is a big, fat zero!

A Monstrous Mother

Greek myths are crammed full of some of the most dangerous, villainous, ugly, horrifying monsters you will find anywhere (although you won't really find them anywhere... because they aren't real, despite what some superstitious teachers might tell you). But one monster stands head and shoulders above all of the others as the worst of the worst.

Echidna, the mother of all monsters. Literally.

Half beautiful woman and half terrifying snake, she lived in a damp, dark cave, slaughtering and eating the ill-fated humans who wandered past, and spending the rest of her time giving birth to her beloved children. Dinosaurs give birth to dinosaurs, humans give birth to humans... so what do monsters give birth to?

Well, Echidna's children include: Cerberus, the many-headed giant dog who guarded Hades; Medusa, the snake-headed woman so ugly that a glance would turn you to stone; the Hydra, the snake-like monster with many heads who, when a head was cut off, would simply grow two more; the Sphinx, the lion with a human head who loved riddles – and killing anyone who got them wrong; the Chimera, a horrid creature who was part-lion, part-goat, part-snake. You get the picture...

Even as a T-rex, I'd feel pretty threatened with brothers and sisters like that!

Theseus was a Greek who not only famously killed a Minotaur, but was also a hero who ruled Athens and Greece incredibly well. Along the way, like other Greek heroes such as Hercules and Perseus, Theseus had to prove his worth in a very dangerous series of adventures. While you will probably have heard of his battle with the Minotaur, your teacher almost certainly won't know these stories:

Procrustes was a fine innkeeper. He took weary travellers in off the road and gave them the finest food and drink, with wonderful entertainment for their pleasure. After dinner, Procrustes would tell the traveller about his special bed. 'It's magic,' he would say. 'No matter how tall you are, I promise that it will be exactly the right size for you – not too long and not too short.'

The traveller would be led to the bed, told to lie down, and then tied up. If he was too tall for the bed, Procrustes would simply chop his legs off. If he was too small, he would be stretched by the limbs until he was tall enough. Either way, by the time it was morning the traveller would certainly be dead. Until, that is, one evening, when Theseus was strapped to the bed. Once he realised what was happening, he flexed his muscles, broke his bonds

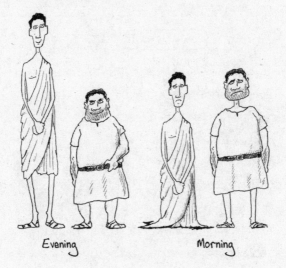

Evening   Morning

and grabbed Procrustes, before tying *him* to the bed and giving him a taste of his own medicine.

Sinis was a bandit who would ambush travellers on the road to Athens and ask for their help bending a pair of pine trees. (This is where I get confused by this myth. You humans do many things that I cannot understand, but bending pine trees? I don't know how Sinis managed to convince these travellers that was a normal thing to do.) With the traveller's help, Sinis would bend the trees

Give me a hand!

until their tips touched the ground and then, quick as a flash, grab some rope and tie the traveller's hands to the trees.

While the traveller could hold them down, he was safe. But as he got more tired, the trees would start to unbend until... RRRIIIPPP! The trees would fling themselves back upright and the traveller would be brutally ripped in two with guts and gore flying everywhere. That is, until Sinis tried his tricks on Theseus, and once again, Theseus managed to turn the tables on his attacker. RRRIIIPPP! And that was the end of Sinis.

Chinese

The Chinese New Year

Nian was a beast who looked a bit like a giant lion with a horned head, enormous teeth and a habit of devouring villagers in China. He lived deep in the ocean and came out once a year to have his annual feast – he would eat farm animals and humans, but his absolute favourite was little children.

On that day, year after year, all the villages along the coast of China would be evacuated to the mountains to try and escape from the destruction Nian caused, but each time he devastated their villages, and snapped up any humans he could find cowering away from him.

One year, an old man refused to flee to the mountains and stayed behind to face Nian on his own. The other villagers thought he was suicidal, but he had a plan. When Nian came, he saw the old man all by himself and thought he had found a nice little appetizer to start

his night with. Quick as a flash, the man threw down firecrackers and shot fireworks into the sky.

It turned out Nian had two fatal weaknesses... The first was loud noises and bright flashes, so he was already on the back foot. The other was, believe it or not, the colour red, and this was the old man's second trick. He unfurled a red banner and waved it in Nian's face, just like a Spanish matador does with a bull. Unlike a bull, the Nian took one look, turned on his claws, and scarpered.

When the villagers returned they were amazed to find their villages untouched and the old man chilling out, completely unharmed. Every year, people all through China hold festivities on that day – now called the Chinese New Year – to celebrate the passing of Nian (whose name, conveniently, translates as 'year'). They still light fireworks and fly red flags and banners... just in case Nian ever tries to show his horned face ever again.

China is a big place – a really big place – and naturally there are a huge number of Chinese myths and traditions... and especially mythological creatures. The Nian is one of the most dangerous of them, but he's got some serious competition:

The Bashe was half-python and half-dragon. At the best of times, snakes aren't the sorts of animals you want to run into (I quite like them actually. I find snake meat makes a delicious little starter). But the Bashe was a snake that even I would try very hard to avoid. It was so big that it was known to eat whole elephants. They would take so long to digest that the Bashe would only spit the bones back out three years later.

Gong Gong was an evil Chinese god who tried to destroy the world, and all the humans in it, with a giant flood. But that's another story. His champion monster was Xiangliu, another colossal snake with not one but nine heads, and when Gong Gong was destroyed Xiangliu went on an angry rampage through China, determined to destroy as much of the world as he could in retaliation for his master's defeat.

To make matters worse, Xiangliu was so bitter and twisted that everywhere he went, after he devastated the towns and villages, the countryside was transformed into a land of poisonous swamps. Fortunately, you won't find him or his nine heads wandering around rural China now. Yu, a famous warrior a bit like Hercules, tracked him down and lopped off each of his heads in a fierce and lengthy battle.

The Kun Peng made the Bashe and the Xiangliu look as tiny as you humans do standing next to me. This beast was a shape-shifter who could either take the shape of a fish (a Kun) or a bird (a Peng). It's impossible to know how big the Kun Peng is, but when it's in the shape of a bird it travels 3,000 miles with one flap of its wings, and it can fly for six months without needing a rest.

If you've never seen one, that might be because they are sky-blue with wings that look like clouds. Or it might be because they are make-believe...

Dangerous Deities

As well as mythological creatures, the Chinese had a lot of gods to think about too, most of whom looked out for the average human and tried to make their lives better. Ch'eng Huang, for example, was the god of the city walls, who protected the village or town you lived in from attackers, and even better, from the God of Death, who would come and take your souls off to the underworld if the Ch'eng Huang couldn't stop it.

But even though the Chinese gods were normally helpful, they would also be very quick to punish bad behaviour. Lei Kung was a human with blue skin, wings, claws and the head of a bird. He was the God of Thunder and had a huge hammer to make thunder-claps with. He often used the great claps of thunder to chase away evil spirits, but he also combined with his wife Lei Zi, the Goddess of Lightning, to punish criminals who had got away with their crimes with some deadly electric justice!

Werewolves seem dangerous enough, but the Chinese have had to contend with something even more worrying... the Weretigers. These creatures were exactly what they sound like – humans who have been cursed or bitten and shape-shift to become ruthless man-eating tigers. The big difference between Werewolves and Weretigers is that Weretigers don't get affected by the full moon. Instead, they transform because of the malevolent curses put on them by evil spirits. But to be honest, if you were one of their victims you probably wouldn't have time to care about all that.

There are many Chinese dragons scattered throughout the land, but fortunately you don't need to be scared of these mythological creatures. In fact, the Chinese dragons were revered and praised, and generally seen as symbols of power and royalty (for example, successful emperors were often seen as having the close support of friendly dragons).

Rather than destroying villages, burning innocent humans to a crisp and chomping on the ones that avoid the fire, these dragons had a variety of jobs in Chinese mythology, including: creating life-giving wind and rain, guarding the gods, protecting hidden treasure  and teaching humans how to write. They seem almost as helpful as a brainy T-rex with a fantastic learnatorium!

Scottish

There are few things more Scottish than haggis, bagpipes and the Loch Ness Monster, affectionately known as Nessie. There are millions of people all over the world who believe that the Monster really exists… which, to my mind, just confirms how daft some humans can be!

Although there was the occasional sighting of a monstrous creature in Loch Ness throughout history, the modern myth of Nessie only started in 1933 when there were two separate sightings of a creature with a large body and a long neck, walking across the road before diving into the Loch. It was unlike any other form of animal seen before. Since then, there have been many more 'sightings', and occasionally Nessie has even been photographed and filmed.

Unfortunately, most of these photos have been proved to be fake, and science has conclusively proved that the Loch Ness Monster simply can't exist for a variety of reasons (like a lack of food supply) but that doesn't stop Nessie fanatics from believing in it. They have even paid for expensive sonar expeditions that have examined the entirety of the Loch a number of times and found... nothing!

It turns out that the Loch Ness Monster is surprisingly just like every other mythological creature in the world: not real.

The Redcaps are much more interesting (and deadly) than the Loch Ness Monster. They are little goblin-like creatures that make their homes in the ruins of castles and forts in rural Scotland. The Redcaps rarely venture out from their lairs, but if a traveller decides to shelter for the night in their vicinity, then they can expect serious trouble... the Redcaps are so called because they dye their hats in their victims' blood! And they never miss an opportunity, because legend has it that if their caps ever go dry, the Redcap dies.

The Terrible Legend of Sawney Bean

Sawney Bean was born in the 1500s, married and decided the honest life wasn't for him. Instead he took his wife, his children, and eventually his many grandchildren and great-grandchildren, to a hidden cave in a cliff. For twenty-five years the Beans lived there, undiscovered.

Their hiding place was a very good one – the cave stretched over a mile into the cliff with many dark twists and turns to pass through. And it had to be, because the Beans didn't go to the shop for their food and drink. Instead, they crept stealthily out at night and, led by Sawney, ambushed innocent travellers and local villagers, killing them before dragging them back to their horrible lair where they devoured their flesh and drank their blood.

Over time, the gruesome family grew until there were forty-eight Beans running around the dark Scottish countryside, waylaying unfortunate Scots for their dinner. Of course, forty-eight humans eat a lot of food, almost as much as one T-rex, so it wasn't surprising that the local Scots soon realised something fishy was going on. However, even though they searched and searched they couldn't find any trace of the culprits. Worse, suspicion for the crimes fell on the innocent, and many blame-less humans were put to death for murders they had not committed.

One fateful day, twenty-five years after Sawney Bean took his first cannibalistic bite, a husband and wife were travelling home after a long day out. Suddenly, from nowhere they were surrounded by the ugly creatures that the Beans had become, all clawing to pull them from their horses. The husband managed to burst through the melee, but his wife wasn't so lucky... she was pulled from her horse and before her husband's very eyes her guts were ripped out and guzzled down by the hungry Bean family.

Just as the newly-widowed chap was going to get the same treatment, a group of travellers burst onto the scene and the Beans fled before they could be caught in the act.

What they didn't know was that the Scottish villagers had hunting dogs at their disposal. Now that they knew what they were looking for, the dogs quickly led the angry Scots to the Beans' lair... but nothing prepared them for what they were about to see. The cave was littered with the grisly bones of over a thousand victims, left to rot once the Beans had had their fill.

Needless to say, the Beans were arrested and taken away, and the Scots weren't the sort of people to show mercy on a family who had killed at least 1,000 people. The men had their hands and feet chopped off and were left to bleed to death, while the women were burned to death.

Have you ever seen anyone lying for hours by a stream with their mouth open? If so, they were probably being haunted by a Scottish Joint-eater. These (very imaginatively named) fairies would choose a victim to haunt and whenever that person sat down to a meal, the Joint-eater would eat the food themselves, leaving just the ghost of the food for the human. The victim would always be hungry, and eventually starved to death, no matter how much they ate.

The only way to get rid of a Joint-eater is to eat an enormous amount of salted beef and lie by running water with your mouth open, until eventually the Joint-eater becomes so thirsty it jumps into the stream and gets washed away. Next time you want seconds of your favourite puddings, try telling your parents you have a Joint-eater haunting you. I've learned that you humans can be fairly gullible (as this book proves!) so they might just believe you.

The Each Uisge was a beautiful horse that liked to chill out by large bodies of water. If you saw one, you would probably think that this noble horse had escaped from its owner and come to the water-side for a nice, refreshing drink. But you would be wrong.

The Each Uisge acted all friendly – until a human jumped onto their back for a quick ride. Suddenly the Each Uisge would shape-shift into the demented horse-like monster it really was. The human would be stuck to the beast's back like they had been superglued, and the Each Uisge would career into the water until it arrived at the deepest part, where it would watch its victim slowly drown. But it wasn't done there... next it wolfed the human down, bones and all. Everything, in fact, except the liver, which it would let float back to the surface and drift to shore, where it would provide evidence of another person lost to the demon-horse of Scotland. Yet the Each Uisge wasn't the most terrifying horse roaming the countryside of Scotland...

The Nuckelavee was a monstrous fiend from the Orkney Islands. It was a skinless horse-man (it looked like a man riding a horse, but it was in fact all one animal). Because it had no skin, its bloody veins and pale skeleton were exposed for everyone to see – a truly disgusting sight.

Its 'horse' head had one giant red eye, and a huge mouth with breath so bad it was toxic... probably like your smelliest teacher before they've brushed their teeth in the morning. The 'man's' head looked fairly normal, except that it was about ten times bigger than it should

have been... oh, and it was skinless, so the skull and brain were on show.

The Nuckelavee searched out humans to gorge on, spreading disease with its foul breath. If you encountered one there was little chance for survival... unless you were near fresh water. The Nuckelavee couldn't stand being splashed by it, and would do its best to avoid getting wet – definitely a handy fact to know late at night on the Orkney Islands!

Romans

When the Romans took over from the Greeks as the leading civilization in Europe, they also stole something else – the Greek gods! Most of the original gods were simply renamed by the Romans, for example Zeus became Jupiter and Poseidon became Neptune. Sometimes, the Romans didn't even bother with a new name... Apollo, the god of poetry and music, was still Apollo, and Uranus, the father of all of the gods, was still Uranus. Not very imaginative! Nonetheless, the Romans did come up with a few myths and legends of their own.

The Founding of Rome – Part I

The origins of Rome could be traced all the way back to another Greek myth (surprise, surprise... get your own myths, Romans!), the fall of Troy. Aeneas was a great Trojan warrior, but when all was lost (thanks to the horse-shaped battering ram, remember), he was commanded to flee by his leader, Hector. Thanking his lucky stars he was getting out alive, Aeneas fled the burning city with only what he could carry – which wasn't much, because he was already carrying his father on his back.

After a series of adventures, he eventually made it to Italy where it was prophesied that he would found a great city, which he did. This city was of course... Lavinium, as any graduate from my learnatorium could have told you. It wasn't until much later that Rome would be founded.

Tarquin the Proud and Horatius at the Bridge

In 534 BC, Tarquin the Proud became the last of the Roman kings, and he wasn't much good as a king either. His reign didn't get off to the best start, because it is thought he murdered the king before him, his own father-in-law, just to get to the throne! Dinosaurs would never be so barbaric... unless we were hungry... then we might be.

In fact, Tarquin was such a terrible ruler that the people hated him and soon there was a revolt. He was forced to flee his country, and enlisted the help of the Etruscans to try and win back his city. With the Etruscan army behind him, Tarquin felt invincible. There was only one thing stopping him from re-conquering Rome and getting his revenge on the people who threw him out: the Tiber River. And a man named Horatius.

To get to Rome, Tarquin and his army had to cross

the Tiber, and fortunately there was one bridge where he could do just that. The few Roman soldiers who were guarding it saw the enormous army coming and thought all was lost. They had to destroy the bridge to stop them, but there was simply no time.

That was when Horatius stepped up. 'I will guard the bridge. You just worry about destroying it,' he said. So his friends got to work while somehow – and this is where the story gets a little far-fetched – Horatius stood firm against the ENTIRE Etruscan army, chopping down enemy soldiers left, right and centre.

When he finally felt the bridge start to give way, Horatius dived off the side just in the nick of time, and managed to swim back to Rome. The Etruscan army were stranded. They couldn't all swim across the river because they would be sitting ducks for the Roman army. While Tarquin the Proud shouted at them furiously to attack, the Etruscans wandered back home, while Horatius returned to a hero's welcome in Rome! (And so he should, there aren't many people who can say they single-handedly defeated an entire army...)

Tarquin was the last king of Rome, and after that it was ruled as a Republic – the first time in recorded human history that the normal people ruled. Dinosaurs, of course, had been more civilised than this hundreds of millions of years ago, but for some reason human historians rarely count dinosaur records in their history books, which I personally think is extremely rude.

The Tarpeian Rock

Tarpeia was a legendary Roman traitor who, in the eighth century BC, famously opened the gates of Rome to their enemies, the Sabines, who came in and rampaged through the city, massacring many people. Tarpeia herself got her just desserts however, because the Sabines rewarded her by crushing her to death with their shields... not the most pleasant way to go. She was buried in a large cliff near the city centre, and from then on this was called the Tarpeian Rock.

Whenever anyone was found guilty of betraying Rome and sentenced to die, their fate was to be thrown off the Tarpeian Rock to their deaths – another not very pleasant way to go, and a reminder of the first time Rome had been so treacherously let down.

The Founding of Rome – Part II

Lavinium, the city that the Trojan Aeneas had founded, was doing well, and its people were spreading out through the Italian countryside. What's more, a pair of twins who were directly descended from Aeneas (but rumoured to have the god of war, Mars, as their father) were about to have a very lucky escape.

Romulus and Remus's great-uncle Amulius heard a prophecy that the two baby boys would one day overthrow him from his role as king of Lavinium. He obviously didn't want that, so he did what any merciful king would do... he left them for dead, outside in a basket. Luckily for our two heroes, a wolf found them. And even more luckily, the wolf didn't eat them but instead decided to raise them as her own!

So the twins grew up happily as wolves until one day a shepherd named Faustulus found them, and he and his wife took them in, to teach them how to live as humans, not just as wolves. When they became adults, they first returned home to meet a very shocked great-uncle Amulius, who then became even more shocked when they kicked him off his throne.

Not content with just that, the twins decided to found a new city, better than Lavinium, on the spot where

the wolf first found them and took pity on them. The brothers must have got some of their father Mars's hot temper though, because brotherly love soon turned to hatred when they couldn't agree on the exact spot on which to found the city.

They decided to settle the argument in the traditional way siblings have been doing for centuries... with a fight to the death! Romulus defeated and killed Remus and he got his way. What's more, he even got to name the city after himself – Rome. If the fight had gone the other way, it could easily have been called Reme!

The Vikings

When the Vikings invaded Britain around 1,000 years ago, they did more than just loot, rape and pillage in their horned helmets (the Viking helmets, incidentally, are yet another myth. Their helmets never had horns on them). The Vikings also brought a new language, different farming techniques and an entirely new and diverse set of gods and stories around them. Your teachers will probably have heard of some, like Thor, the God of Thunder, with his enormous hammer. But there were a lot of other gods too, and here are just a handful:

Odin, the god of war, death, wisdom and poetry, ruled over all the other gods. He rode a fantastic eight-legged horse and used two ravens to fly over the world and tell him everything that was happening. He was the smartest of all beings, and his desire for learning might even have surpassed my own, the great Dr Dino's. He was once offered the chance to gain infinite wisdom in exchange

for one eye. Without a second thought, he took out his knife and POP! Out came his eye, and in went the intelligence. His son is, in fact, Thor.

Loki was a trickster god, who loved to cause mischief, and there are many tales of his pranks worth hearing, like the time he cut off all of Thor's wife Sif's hair just for fun, or the time he tricked a giant into building the walls of Asgard, where the gods lived. While a lot of his pranks were relatively harmless and amusing (although not if you were the one who ended up a bald goddess!), they did not endear him to two of Odin's other sons...

Hodur was the blind God of Darkness, but of greater significance was his sibling Baldur, the God of Light and Purity, who was liked by all he met and one of the most favoured of all of the many gods. There was one who was jealous of him, however – Loki.

Baldur began having a recurring nightmare that he would die one day. I would have told him to get over it... we're all going to die one day – even me, Dr Dino, the last T-rex on Earth. His mother, however, grew worried and decided to get all of the plants and animals on the planet to swear they wouldn't harm Baldur. This just riled Loki even more... why should Baldur get so much attention because of a bad dream? With a little investigation, he discovered that Baldur's mother hadn't bothered to get mistletoe to swear to protect him.

So, Loki being Loki, he immediately grabbed some mistletoe and made a very sharp spear out of it. Knowing that if he was around, Baldur would be on his guard, Loki then put his masterstroke into action. He gave the spear to Baldur's blind brother Hodur and told him it was time for target practice. He pointed him to the 'target' – his own brother – and told him to let fly. Hodur may have been blind, but he was strong and accurate too, and the spear flew straight and true... right through Baldur! Even gods can't survive that, and he fell down dead immediately.

Yggdrasil and the Norns

The Vikings believed that there were nine inter-connected worlds, and in the centre of all of these was Yggdrasil, the biggest tree it is possible to imagine. The roots of Yggdrasil were buried deep in the underworld, and the branches extended right up into heaven.

Many stories and events occurred at the tree. For example, Odin earned infinite wisdom from a pool of water at its base (although it was also the tree where he would ultimately hang himself!). The tree was also home to a fair amount of wildlife – and I'm not just talking about squirrels! (Although there is a squirrel who lived in the tree and gossiped all day.) A great dragon gnawed at its roots, sucking the blood from dead humans that ended up at the tree, while at the top of the branches lived an enormous eagle, who hated the dragon and who protected the tree from the dragon's powerful and potentially damaging claws.

More importantly, for humans at least, are the three Norns – giant hag-like Goddesses of Fate. These three women lived at the bottom of the tree by another well, the Well of Fate, and they were present every time a human child was born. Straight away, the Norns would play out some thread, and that spinning thread would show the fate of the newborn child. If the thread was snipped, the life would be cut short too!

In order to appease them, a new mother and baby would be served Norn porridge directly after birth. It was a special porridge designed to appease the Norns and grant long life and happiness.

Loki's trouble-making didn't just stop with him. His children were at it too. Even one of the better-behaved daughters, the monstrous goddess Hel, was queen of the icy Norse underworld of Helheim. She ruled over a land full of mist, freezing winds and little else which, once entered, could never be left, by mortal humans and gods alike (dinosaurs excepted, of course).

Another child was the Midgard Serpent, a sea-snake who Thor truly hated. Odin tried to rid the world of the foul creature by chucking it into the vast sea that surrounded Midgard, the world that the humans lived in. Yet the Midgard Serpent bided its time, growing larger and larger, until eventually it was big enough to wrap itself right around the entirety of Midgard. Legend has it that when the Serpent let go, it would cause the end of the world.

But perhaps none were as brutal or deadly as the Fenrir Wolf, a cunning beast that would one day kill Odin, and help to cause the beginning of the end: Ragnarok, the period when the Norse believed that each of the nine worlds would be destroyed.

That Loki certainly likes causing trouble!

English

As has been discussed earlier, King Arthur is really a Welsh legend that the English have stolen and made English. Although, to be fair to the English, most of the stories that you may have heard about Merlin, Lancelot, Gawain, Arthur himself, and the rest of his Knights of the Round Table were invented after Arthur 'became' English.

However, this isn't the only time the English have stolen something foreign to make it their own. What is the most English legend you can think of? How about the patron saint of England, St George himself, and the mighty slaying of the dragon…?

St George and the Dragon

The legend goes that bold St George had travelled far and wide to carry out charitable and holy deeds for whoever needed them. One day he reached Libya, where he heard tell of a horrible dragon living nearby who demanded payment of one young maiden every day to be offered up to be eaten. If he wasn't paid, he would destroy the nearby towns and villages with his awful poisonous breath.

The day that St George arrived, it so happened that the King's daughter had been chosen, and the whole land was in mourning for her certain death. The King himself had offered her hand in marriage to any man who could defeat the dragon – surely a hopeless task. But this is the sort of thing St George lived for.

Strengthening himself with prayers, the knight approached the dragon's lair and charged at it with his lance down. Catching the dragon with a mighty blow, the bold knight thought he had felled the hideous beast. Unfortunately, the dragon was covered in armoured scales and the lance shattered on impact. A powerful battle followed, with the brave knight constantly dodging the dragon's poison and trying to find a way through his defences with his sword (and, bizarrely, taking refuge under an orange tree to catch his breath every so often. Apparently, the dragon hated oranges...)

Finally, he saw a weakness underneath the dragon's wing and he stabbed at it. The blade sunk into the dragon's unprotected stomach, and the dragon was killed. St George saved the day, and got to marry the beautiful princess.

'But wait,' I hear the clever children saying. 'If this happened in Libya, what does it have to do with England? Was St George English?'

Very good questions, children, and the answers are 'nothing' and 'no'. In fact, very little is known about the real St George, but what can be found in my learnatorium tells me that St George was actually born in Turkey in the third century AD and served time as a Roman soldier. He stood up for Christian beliefs, for which he was tortured and killed horribly. Reports vary as to what happened to him, but he was either crushed between two spiked wheels, poisoned, boiled in a vat of molten lead, or beheaded. I'm not sure which I'd prefer myself.

So, the patron saint of England wasn't English, had never been to England, almost certainly couldn't speak English, and quite possibly had never heard of the place either! Even the made-up story about the slaying of the dragon happened in Africa!

England, like all other countries it seems, has its fair share of mythological creatures roaming the country late at night. There are too many to write about here, but if you ever want to visit my learnatorium to find out more, you are more than welcome. Here are a handful:

A Church Grim could come in many forms: a black dog, a small black-skinned goblin, a lamb, a ram, a horse... anything really. Their role was always the same, however. They protected the church they were attached to and everything inside it, kept the place clean and tidy, and loved to mischievously ring the bells right when nobody was expecting it. Their name might have been Grim, but these spirits were really very helpful. Although how a horse or a dog could Hoover is beyond me. I find it hard enough as a dinosaur.

Jack O'Kent was an extremely cunning man who would wander the countryside of England and occasionally

clash with the Devil himself. There are many stories about their battles of wits, but the best one involves a bridge, a bone, and an unlucky dog.

A village desperately needed a bridge to cross a nearby river, but they couldn't afford to build one. They asked Jack O'Kent for help, and he made a deal with the Devil – if he helped Jack build the bridge, then the Devil could take the soul of whoever crossed the bridge first. They shook on it, and the Devil worked away until the bridge had been built in record time. Jack, waiting for his opportunity, spotted a dog and threw a bone across the bridge for the dog to chase. The poor mutt did, and in an instant the animal was killed, its soul travelling to stay with the Devil for all eternity.

The Devil himself was furious at being tricked like this, but there was nothing he could do. He had been bested by Jack O'Kent again.

John Lambton, heir to the Lambton estate, was a naughty young boy and one Sunday he skipped church, heading off instead to do some fishing. Along the way he met an old man who told him that no good would come from skiving off church, but it was a beautiful day so John ignored him. While fishing, John caught a strange eel-like creature, three feet long, slimy and horrible. The old man, who had been watching him, told him he had caught the Devil himself. John thought to himself, 'That old fool is crazy! It's just an eel.' But rather than throw the fish back, he instead tossed it down a nearby well.

Years passed, during which time John forgot all about it and went off to fight in the Crusades. Over time, though, the well grew poisonous, and when the local villagers went to check it out they got a nasty shock. The eel was actually an evil baby dragon, or wyrm as they were called, and had now grown to full size. The Lambton Wyrm, as it came to be known, started terrorising the neighbourhood, eating the farm animals (and any farmers who happened to be in the way!) and killing any knights who tried to fight it.

It turned out that not only was the Wyrm enormous, armoured and poisonous, but it could also regenerate its own flesh after it had been stabbed – a powerful combination of skills which made it extremely deadly.

Eventually John returned to discover the devastation wrought by the Wyrm. The entire region lived in terror of the beast, and when John realised he was responsible for the monster, he was devastated. He decided he must be the one to defeat the Wyrm, but first went to see a wise woman for advice.

The wise woman told him to cover his armour in spikes and fight the Wyrm in the river Wear, where he originally fished it from. If he did that, he would have a chance of surviving, although there was one condition. He had to kill the first living thing he saw after his victory, or else his entire family would be cursed for nine generations.

John did everything the woman said and prepared for battle. A deadly fight followed, and the Wyrm quickly went for its favourite finishing move: squeezing the knight until he popped. But as it wrapped itself around the knight it cut itself horribly on his spikes, and as the chunks of flesh were cut off they fell into the river, floating away so that they couldn't regenerate and heal. After hours of battle, the Wyrm was finally dead.

John wasn't dumb. He had arranged that after the battle his father should release their pet dog which would come running up to John so that John could kill it. Unfortunately, John's father *was* dumb. He was so excited that he completely forgot and ran up to John himself to congratulate him.

John knew he had to kill his father... but he couldn't. Which, it turns out, was the wrong thing to do in the long run, because for nine generations each of the Lambtons died gruesome deaths.

Most would say the moral of that story is 'Don't skip church...', but in my opinion the moral should be: Don't use stupid people as part of an important plan!

Quiz

1. Why did Anubis, the Egyptian God of Death, have a jackal's head?

   A. It was a punishment for ill-deeds in a past life; B. His jackal's nose was useful for sniffing out dead people; C. Jackals were good guards, and he guarded grave-yards; D. Jackals were known for digging up graves in cemeteries.

2. Why are Scottish Redcaps called Redcaps?

   A. Because they are bald and are constantly sun-burned, so it looks like they are wearing red caps; B. They dye their caps in the blood of their victims; C. It's an ironic name – they actually wear blue caps; D. Their caps are constantly wet from the Scottish rain, and the colour has run from their ginger hair over the years, dying the caps red.

3. What was the Greeks' wooden horse at Troy, really?
   A. A real horse; B. A huge catapult that fired horses at the defenders of Troy; C. A wooden cow that the Greeks hid in; D. A battering ram in the shape of a horse.

4. How can you escape from the Japanese creature Aka Manto?
   A. Throw toilet water in his face; B. Ask for all the toilet paper he has; C. Say you don't need any toilet paper; D. Moon him.

5. How did the wicked Greek Sinis kill his victims?
   A. He tied them to the top of a tree, pulled it back and then used it to catapult them for miles; B. He tied them to a tree, rubbed them in honey and waited for bears to come and eat them; C. He pulled a tree out of the ground and used it as a club to smash the victims into the ground; D. He tied them to two trees and used them to rip the victims apart.

6. What did Maui catch that became the North Island of New Zealand?
   A. A dreadful cold, which caused him to sneeze up the entire island; B. An enormous fish; C. A

dangerous sea-dragon; D. A big bit of drift-wood, which he carved into the island.

7. What happened to Ancient Egyptians that killed a cat?
A. They were turned into a cat by the Sphinx; B. They were put to death themselves; C. They were given a great reward, as cats were a pest. The bigger the cat, the bigger the reward; D. They were forced to eat the cat whole.

8. What happened to the German child Augustus, who refused to eat his soup?
A. His parents made him fish and chips instead; B. He was so hungry that, after a couple of days, he ate all of the soup in the house and his stomach exploded; C. He starved to death; D. He lived a long and happy life – soup-free.

9. Why did the Aztecs practise human sacrifice by ripping out the victims' hearts and throwing their bodies down a pyramid?
A. To recreate the way Huitzilpochtli killed his half-sister; B. It seemed like the most sensible way to kill some-one at the time; C. They took bets on how big

the heart was; D. They took bets on how many times the body would bounce on the way down the pyramid *and* how big the heart was.

10. What did the Welsh Canrig Bwt like to eat?
A. Frogs and insects; B. The brains of children; C. The blood of another living thing; D. Soup.

11. How was the Chinese monster Nian driven away?
A. A brave knight attacked it and forced it to flee; B. A bigger monster came and scared it off; C. By an old man armed with fireworks and red banners; D. By the Chinese Emperor himself.

12. Why did Fionn MacCumhail pretend to be his own baby child?
A. To trick Benandonner into thinking he was much bigger than he really was; B. He liked sucking on dummies; C. He was preparing for a major movie role where he played a baby trapped in a giant's body; D. He was playing a game of hide-and-seek with the other Irish giants.

13. Romulus founded Rome. What happened to Remus?
A. He was killed by his brother in an argument over where to found Rome; B. He founded Reme, which was later destroyed in battle by the Romans; C. He decided city-building wasn't for him and became a shepherd instead; D. He outlived his brother and became the second king of Rome.

14. The Norns were the three Viking goddesses who lived at the bottom of Yggdrasil. What were they in charge of?
A. Making sure the tree Yggdrasil stayed standing; B. They were Loki's babysitters to make sure he didn't get into too much trouble. There had to be three of them because he was so mischievous; C. Feeding the rest of the gods… a full-time job! D. The fates of all humans.

15. What is a weakness of the Japanese creatures the Kappa?
A. Cucumbers; B. They are too polite; C. Water spilling from the cup on the top of their head; D. All of the above.

16. What is the only way to defeat the Abhartach, the Irish vampire-dwarf?

    A. Drive a stake through its heart; B. Bury it upside-down; C. Behead it; D. Feed it so much blood that it gets too full and dies of obesity.

17. What does the Each Uisge, the Scottish demon horse, do with its victims?

    A. Drowns them and then eats them; B. Runs off a cliff with them strapped to its back; C. Bites off their heads; D. Transports them to the under-world.

18. What did the Romans do with the Tarpeian Rock?

    A. Throw traitors off of it to execute them; B. Kiss it for luck; C. Use it to tell their fortunes; D. Use it to smash other rocks into smaller rocks.

19. Where is St George from?

    A. London; B. Yorkshire; C. Turkey; D. China.

20. What happens to German children who suck their thumbs too much?

    A. Nothing. B. Their parents cover their thumbs in blood to stop them sucking them. C. Their thumbs are cut off with a pair of scissors; D. Their hands are tied to their legs until they can stop.

Answers

1.	D	8.	C	15.	D
2.	B	9.	A	16.	B
3.	D	10.	B	17.	A
4.	C	11.	C	18.	A
5.	D	12.	A	19.	C
6.	B	13.	A	20.	C
7.	B	14.	D		

Also available in this series:

How Fast Can You Fart?

The wildest, weirdest, funniest, grossest, fastest, longest, brainiest and best facts about history, science, food geography, words, and much more!
ISBN: 978 1 78219 766 9
£5.99

Did Romans Really Wash Themselves in Wee?

The wackiest, wittiest, filthiest, foulest, oldest, wisest and best facts about history!
ISBN: 978 1 78219 915 1
£5.99

Do Turtles Really Breathe Out of Their Bums?

The funniest, grossest and most amazing facts about all kinds of favourite animals!
ISBN: 978 1 78219 774 4
£5.99

How Do Astronauts Wee in Space?

The wildest, weirdest, funniest, filthiest, wisest, grossest, brainiest and best facts about space!
ISBN: 978 1 78418 653 1
£5.99

Do Dinosaurs Make Good Pets?

The wackiest, wisest, grossest, brainiest, oldest and best facts about the prehistoric world!
ISBN 978 1 78418 652 4
£5.99